92
WIN
    Woods, Geraldine
        The Oprah Winfrey
    story

DATE DUE			
JAN 1 8 1994			
NOV 8 1996			
DEC 3 1997			

The Oprah Winfrey Story

Speaking Her Mind

An Authorized Biography

Geraldine Woods

DILLON PRESS, INC.
Minneapolis, Minnesota 55415

Photographic Acknowledgments

The photographs are reproduced through the courtesy of Steve Fenn; Jorie Gracen/London Features International; HARPO Productions, Inc. (© HARPO/Kingworld); Paul Natkin; Ron Slenzak; Oprah Winfrey; and Ron Wolfson/London Features International. Cover by Paul Natkin. A special thanks to the staff at HARPO Productions and Oprah Winfrey for their generous cooperation and assistance.

Library of Congress Cataloging-in-Publication Data

Woods, Geraldine.
  The Oprah Winfrey Story : speaking her mind / Geraldine Woods.
    p. cm. — (Taking part)
  Includes bibliographical references and index.
  Summary: A biograghy of talk show host Oprah Winfrey, the first woman to ever own her own talk show and the first black woman to own her own production company.
  ISBN 0-87518-463-4
  1. Winfrey, Oprah—Juvenile literature. 2. Television personalities—United States—Biography. 3. Motion picture actors and actresses—United States—Biography. 4. Television personalities. [1. Winfrey, Oprah. 2. Afro-Americans—Biography. 3. Actors and actresses.] I. Title.
PN1992.4.W56W66   1991
791.45' 082' 092—dc20
[B]   91-7818
                                                                          CIP
                                                                          AC

Dillon Press, Inc., 242 Portland Avenue South
Minneapolis, Minnesota 55415

Printed in the United States of America
1 2 3 4 5 6 7 8 9 10 99 98 97 96 95 94 93 92 91

About the Author

Geraldine Woods has written many books for children on a variety of subjects. For this biography, she interviewed Oprah Winfrey to gain a firsthand knowledge of the famous television and film star and successful business-woman.

Ms. Woods has written several Dillon Press books, including Taking Part biographies of Jim Henson and Bill Cosby, a People in Focus biography of Sandra Day O'Connor, and a Heritage book about Spain. She has taught at private and public schools in New York City, and is a longtime New York resident.

Contents

"The Oprah Winfrey Show" is seen by more than fifteen million people each day.

1

Making Up Stories and Characters

The host sits on a gray plush rug. The hot lights of the television studio brighten her red jacket and dark, shining hair. She's only there for a moment. Soon she bounces to her feet and almost runs across the floor to bring the microphone to a guest. "Let's talk about that," she says to a mother who comments about raising children. "That's important."

For a few minutes during the hour-long show, she sits on a raised platform with her guest, an expert in child care. Most of the time she roams through the audience. To her, the ideas of ordinary people are as valuable as those of the famous. From time to time, she breaks into the discussion with her own comments—stories about her childhood, her friends, her godchildren. She is anything but formal. She hugs one guest, pats another, and even stops to fix one woman's hair. "You're on national TV," she explains. "You want to look nice."

Her hair is sprayed gray, and one eye is taped almost shut. On her face are scars applied by a clever makeup artist. But no cream or powder created the look of suffering on her face. That comes from the actress. The character she is playing is Sofia, a black woman beaten and jailed because she dared to consider herself equal to whites. For two days the actress has been sitting at a dinner table waiting as the director focuses on others in the scene. She is thinking of Fannie Lou Hamer, a civil rights worker who spent many long months in jail for protesting racial injustices. She plans her speech to display Fannie Lou's courage and strength. Finally it is her

Oprah has won acclaim for her acting roles.

turn. "I set in that jail 'til I near about rot to death," she says. "I know what it's like to want to sing and have it beat out of you."

The woman sits in her living room surrounded by young girls who come from a housing project where the poorest people in Chicago live. She has adopted them as her "little sisters." They see her often, receiving support, help with schoolwork, and advice about life. She is loving, but strict with them. "Get pregnant and I'll break your face!" she says. "You want something to love, tell me and I'll buy you a puppy." She urges them to study. "Don't tell me you want to do great things in your life if all you carry to school is a radio."

☆ ☆ ☆

These three women—the actress, the television host, and the big sister—are really just one person.

Oprah Winfrey is the star of "The Oprah Winfrey Show," the nation's most popular talk show. Each "Oprah Winfrey Show" is seen by about 15 million people in more than 200 American cities and three foreign countries. Oprah is also the actress who played Sofia in the film *The Color Purple*. She received an Oscar nomination for that performance. Most importantly, she is a concerned citizen, who uses her talent, fame, and wealth to help others. As if these jobs were not enough to occupy her time, Oprah also runs a multimillion dollar movie and television production company, HARPO Productions, Inc. (Read the letters backwards to find out why Oprah chose that name.) Oprah also created and starred in a television miniseries, "The Women of Brewster Place."

Oprah Winfrey is certainly one of the busiest women in the world. She is probably also one of the wealthiest and most famous. But Oprah wasn't born at the top. She had to travel there from a little farm in Kosciusko, Mississippi.

Oprah Gail Winfrey was born on January 29, 1954. Her father, Vernon Winfrey, was a soldier on leave when he met eighteen-year-old Vernita Lee. They were together only a short time, and were never married. When Vernon returned to Fort Rucker, he didn't even know that Vernita was expecting a baby.

Vernita had planned to call her child *Orpah*, a name from the Book of Ruth in the Bible. However, the midwife made a mistake when she recorded the birth, switching the *R* and the *P*. Because of this error, *Oprah* became the baby's official name.

Soon after her daughter's birth, Vernita went to Milwaukee, Wisconsin, to seek work as a maid. She left Oprah on the family farm with her parents. Oprah's grandparents, Hattie Mae and Henry Lee, led a simple life. Their old, three-room house didn't

Two-year-old Oprah on the steps of grandmother's house.

Oprah, her mother, and her older cousin.

Hattie Mae.

Vernon and Oprah.

even have indoor plumbing. The only water came from a well about a hundred yards away. When Oprah was old enough, one of her daily chores was to draw enough water from the well for the family washing and cooking. Oprah also fed the pigs and took the cows to pasture each day.

The lonely farm girl had few toys. "I didn't have a television," Oprah explains. "I entertained myself, making up stories and characters. I read whatever books I could get my hands on. I talked to myself."

Hattie Mae, the grandmother whom Oprah called "Momma," had taught the intelligent child to read and write at the age of three. She was strict but loving. Whenever Oprah was naughty, Momma hit her with a small branch—which Oprah had to fetch from a tree herself! "I used to get whipped every day," Oprah recalls, "but I am what I am because of my grandmother. My strength, my sense of reasoning...all of that was set by the time I was six years old."

Hattie Mae also gave Oprah a firm religious upbringing. Oprah recalls the Sunday schedule: "You did Sunday school, you did the morning services, which started at 11:00 and didn't end until 2:30. You had dinner on the ground in front of the church, and then you'd go back in for the 4:00 service."

Oprah also remembers getting an important lesson on the meaning of life from Hattie Mae. "I was four, watching my grandma boil clothes in a huge iron pot. I was crying, and Grandma asked, 'What's the matter with you, girl?'

'Big Mammy,' I sobbed, 'I'm going to die someday.'

'Honey,' she said, 'God doesn't mess with His children. You got a lot of work to do in your life and not be afraid. The strong have got to take care of the other.'"

Oprah believes that although she was very young, her grandmother's words took root in her. "I knew I was going to help people, that I had a higher calling."

Today, Oprah continues to admire Hattie Mae's faith. Oprah reads a verse of the Bible every day and prays every night. "I get down on my knees and pray," she says. "I feel incomplete without it." Oprah explains that when her grandmother first taught her to pray, Momma said, "As long as you have the power to bow your head and bend your knees, you do it and God will hear you better." Oprah adds, "I'll look like [Momma] when I'm old. I'll be one of those spiritual ladies rockin' and shoutin' in church."

The Kosciusko Baptist Church was the scene of Oprah's first public performance. From the age of three, young "Mistress Winfrey" often recited poetry for the congregation. Oprah says, "I'd have these little, little patent leather shoes. Oh, very proper."

Four-year-old Oprah's yearbook picture.

With a friend at Christmas.

Oprah's fifth birthday party.

With her step-mother Zelma, an aunt, and a younger cousin.

Oprah's audience grew each year. "I spoke for every women's group, banquet, church function. I did the circuit." She also used her public speaking skills in school—to survive. In first grade six classmates threatened to beat her up. Oprah "...told them about Jesus of Nazareth and what happened to the people who tried to stone him. The kids called me The Preacher and left me alone after that."

Oprah's classmates may have picked on her because they were jealous of her brains. Oprah wrote this note to her kindergarten teacher: "Dear Miss New. I do not think I belong here." Miss New, whose students were just about to learn the alphabet, agreed. She skipped Oprah into the first grade. After the first grade, Oprah skipped to third. She explains, "I was always the smartest kid in class and that worked for me...I was the one who would read the assignment early and turn in the paper ahead of time."

Oprah's success in school was soon overshadowed by personal troubles. When her daughter reached the age of six, Vernita took Oprah to live with her in Milwaukee. Vernita had had another child, Patricia, and she wanted Oprah to join her. However, Vernita found it difficult to be a single parent. A year later, Vernon invited Oprah to live with him and his new wife Zelma in Nashville. Vernita agreed.

Oprah was very happy with her father and stepmother. Unfortunately, her stay with them lasted only a year. Then Vernita decided to try again with her young daughter. Vernita was engaged to be married, and she had another new baby, this time a boy named Jeffrey. It seemed like a good time to reunite with her first child and to form a new family.

This was the beginning of a stormy period in Oprah's life.

Oprah wearing the glasses that would get her into a lot of trouble.

Looking For Love in All the Wrong Places

Melinda and Sandy—those were the two pets that Oprah kept in her mother's tiny apartment in Milwaukee. They weren't dogs or cats or even goldfish. Vernita's salary as a part-time maid, and the welfare benefits she sometimes received, barely covered necessary items such as food and rent. Pets did not fit into the budget. But Oprah wanted a pet, and she was not a person who gave up easily. She caught a pair of cockroaches and kept them in a jar.

A few years later, Oprah saved enough money to buy a tiny French poodle, which she named Simone. Soon, Oprah explains, "My mother threatened to give him away for pooping on the floor." Once again, Oprah refused to give up. "I thought if I could make the puppy look like a hero, I'd get to keep it." So Oprah opened all the drawers and threw her mother's jewelry out the window. She told Vernita that when she arrived home, she found the house in that condition and that "Simone was chasing three men down the stairs." Vernita was not fooled. She had seen Oprah's imagination at work before. A huge mother/daughter battle followed—one of many during Oprah's pre-teen years.

Oprah's desire for new glasses caused another dramatic argument. Oprah had a pair of "butterfly" frames that she hated. She wanted a newer, more fashionable style. Vernita told her daughter that there was no money. So Oprah faked a robbery and trampled her glasses. When the police arrived, Oprah was "unconscious." Later at the hospital she "awoke" but found that she had "lost" her memory. Vernita, sobbing, asked the police if anything else had been damaged in the apartment. "Just a pair of glasses," replied the officer.

Vernita stared at her daughter. The look on her mother's face inspired Oprah to "regain" her memory. She made a very quick recovery! And she did get a new pair of glasses.

There were other incidents. Once Oprah ran away from home. She saw Aretha Franklin, the famous singer, and told her that she needed $100 to get back to Ohio. Aretha gave her the money. Oprah spent the next three days in a hotel in downtown Milwaukee, ordering food from room service and enjoying the luxury, until the money ran out. Then, frightened and weeping, she went to her minister, who brought her home.

Why did Oprah do these things? Probably there were a number of reasons. Oprah has always been extremely creative and determined. Those qualities

Nine-year-old Oprah with her mother, half-sister Patricia, and half-brother Jeffrey, in Milwaukee.

can bring success—as they eventually did—but only if they are channeled in the right direction. At that early age, Oprah did not know how to focus her energy. All too often, Vernita did not know how to guide her headstrong daughter, either. Vernita had to cope with her own problems. She was poor, had two other children, and a new relationship with a man.

Oprah remembers watching "Leave it to Beaver," a television comedy. The parents were perfect. The mother stayed home in a spotlessly clean house and devoted herself completely to her children. Whenever there was a crisis, the parents sat down and talked to their children. No one was ever angry for long, and all problems were solved at the end of the half-hour. "Leave it to Beaver" was not a real-life story, but Oprah yearned for that type of family life. "I wanted my mother to have cookies ready for me [when I came home from school] and to say, 'How was your day?' But she was one of the maids. And she was tired."

Today, Oprah understands her mother better. "She was just trying to survive. Her way of showing love to me was getting out and going to work every day, putting clothes on my back, and having food on the table." Oprah adds, "My mother did the most she

In the 1960's Oprah was discouraged by the differences between her life
and those of white families on television. Now she makes shows about black
families—like The Women of Brewster Place.

could." That is Oprah's adult view. But at the time, the differences between her life and television's view of family life made Oprah resentful. She acted out her anger, and by doing so she got herself into trouble.

Adding to her pain was the fact that when Oprah was only nine years old, she was raped by a nineteen-year-old cousin. Other men also sexually abused her during her childhood. Oprah was terribly frightened by these experiences. Like all young children, she enjoyed affection. She had a right to expect loving attention from the adults in her life. When the attention became sexual, she was powerless to prevent it. She did not even completely understand what was happening to her.

Even though she was an innocent victim, Oprah felt guilty. Her cousin took her to the zoo and bought her ice cream, bribing her to keep quiet. He need not have worried. Oprah explains, "I didn't tell anybody about it because I thought I would be blamed for it."

Oprah was also worried about pregnancy. She had only a vague understanding of her body. Throughout the fifth grade, she was afraid she was going to have a baby. "Every time I had a stomachache I thought I was pregnant and asked to go to the bathroom so if I had it [the baby] no one could see," says Oprah. "That for me was the terror: Was I going to have it? How would I hide it? All the people would be mad at me! How could I keep it in my room without my mother knowing it?"

Today Oprah realizes that she should have told someone. Every child has a right to control his or her own body. Anyone who is touched in a way that feels uncomfortable should ask an adult—a relative, friend, or teacher—for help.

Oprah tried to cope with these problems all by herself. She says now that after her abuse she began

"...looking for love in all the wrong places." Oprah dated anyone who was willing, bringing boys home when Vernita was out. Because she felt guilty about the sexual abuse, she did not respect herself. Therefore, few boys respected her.

In 1968, at the age of thirteen, Oprah faced a new challenge. She transferred to Nicolet High School in Fox Point, a suburb of Milwaukee. A teacher in the inner-city school Oprah had been attending noticed her reading during lunch hour. "My teachers started talking to me, saying, 'You need to get out of this environment.'" Oprah's new school, an expensive private institution, gave her a scholarship as she entered the ninth grade. At Nicolet, Oprah comments, "I was the only black kid, and I mean the only one." The other students were upper-middle class, suburban, and white. "I would take the bus in the morning with the maids who worked in their homes."

Oprah and Vernita gradually learned to get along.

Still, Oprah says she did not feel out of place in her high school. "I've never felt out of place anywhere," she says. "I've felt outnumbered many times. There's a big difference." The difference lies, Oprah believes, in "...knowing you can do the work, whatever the work is. The difference is knowing you can excel.

What made me know is education. I always knew I could outread, outwrite, outtalk anybody. So I never felt unequal to anybody."

Yet Nicolet was a difficult experience in some ways. Oprah continues, "I realized I was poor then...As long as no one tells you otherwise, and you don't see the other side, you're O.K. But in that new school I felt unimportant and insecure. So I'd make up stories and lie to the kids about what my parents did."

Oprah felt very alone, and she grew more delinquent. One day her mother had enough. Vernita took Oprah to a detention center for teenage girls. However, all the beds were filled, and the authorities told Vernita to return in two weeks. Vernita had reached her limit; two weeks were too long. Once again, she sent Oprah to her father's home in Nashville. That move saved Oprah's life.

Oprah was elected "Most Popular" by her senior class in Nashville.

3

I Want To Be a Journalist

Vernon Winfrey had established himself as a solid citizen of Nashville in the years after Oprah's birth. He owned a barbershop and served as city councillor. When Oprah returned to live with him and her stepmother Zelma, they had no children of their own. But Vernon Winfrey's barbershop, which he still owns, displays a sign: "Attention teenagers. If you are tired of being hassled by unreasonable parents, now is the time for action. Leave home and pay your own way while you still know everything." That mixture of humor and self-confidence was typical of Vernon Winfrey. It allowed him to take charge of Oprah firmly and lovingly.

Oprah arrived in Nashville wearing heavy makeup

and revealing clothing. Her behavior was out of control. Vernon immediately scrubbed the makeup off his daughter's face. He ordered her to change her clothes, and gave her a strict curfew. When Oprah called him "Pops," Vernon told her, "I was 'Daddy' when you left and I'm going to be 'Daddy' since you're back. I will not accept the word 'Pops!'" Oprah called him "Daddy" after that.

From the moment she arrived, Vernon established himself as the boss. Most of the time, to discipline Oprah he only had to use "the look" that his dad had used on him. He put his chin on his chest and stared out of the corner of his eye at Oprah. Sometimes "the look" wasn't enough. His physical punishment fell into two categories—"whippin" and "whoopin." "Whoopin" was the more severe; luckily he never had to "whoop" Oprah.

Vernon and Zelma appealed to her intelligence

instead. They returned to a practice they had begun during Oprah's first stay in Nashville. Oprah was required to learn five new words a day and write book reports. At first she read a book a week, and later five books every two weeks. When she brought home a report card with Cs on it, Vernon scolded her. Oprah protested that Cs weren't really bad grades. Vernon answered, "If you were a child who could only get Cs, then that is all I would expect of you. But you are not. And so in this house, for you, Cs are not acceptable."

As an adult, Oprah says "...the most important thing my father did for me was exude [show] a belief in himself that I knew I could not override. I could not get away with anything, because when my father said something, he absolutely meant it." Vernon stated his view of authority another way: "If I tell you a mosquito can pull a wagon, don't ask me no questions. Just hitch him up!"

Oprah's life began to improve. She became an honor student at Nashville's East High School. There she was again one of only a few black students. Oprah joined the drama club and won an award for her speeches. At sixteen she was voted the most popular girl in the class. She was also elected president of the student council, running on the slogan, "Vote for the Grand Ole Oprah." In 1970, she was chosen because of her excellent grades and extracurricular activities to represent her high school at the White House Conference on Youth in Estes Park, Colorado. More important than recognition for her accomplishments was the respect Oprah gained for herself.

With her personal life more in order, Oprah took steps on the road to her future career. At the age of seventeen, she entered a beauty contest for "Miss Fire Prevention." She was sponsored by a local black radio station, WVOL. Oprah comments, "I know it's not

Oprah with her bosses at WVOL Radio, Nashville.   *Senior yearbook picture.*

a biggie, but I was...the first black to win the darned thing."

On the day of the Miss Fire Prevention contest, Oprah turned on the television and watched Barbara Walters, a famous television interviewer. When the contest judge inquired about her future plans, Oprah had intended to say she wanted to be a fourth grade teacher. But instead she replied, "I believe in truth, so I want to be a journalist."

After the contest, Oprah stopped at the radio station that had sponsored her to pick up her prizes, a wristwatch and a clock. One of the engineers asked her if she would like to hear her voice on tape. As Oprah read the news into the microphone, a group of station employees gathered to listen. She sounded great! Soon afterward, she became an employee herself—a news announcer. Each day after school, she went to WVOL to read the news, every half hour until 8:30.

By her senior year in high school, Oprah had a great job, terrific grades, lots and lots of friends...and an eleven o'clock curfew. It's not surprising that she wanted to go away to college. Vernon and Zelma, on the other hand, wanted her with them a little longer.

ALABAMA ELKDOM

(Gertrude Crum Sanders -- Reporter)

REGION V
Oratorical contestants - July 26, 1970 - Montgomery, Alabama. Reading from left to right, Solomon G. Tyler, student from Alces Fortier High School, New Orleans, La.; Earnestine Naomi Dixon, student from Immaculate Conception High School, Clarksdale, Mississippi; Richard N. Callow, student from St. Anthony Seminary High School, San Antonio, Texas; Dianne Craig, student from Central High School, Mobile, Alabama; Jay Thomas Youngdahl, student ⌐ Hall High School, Little Rock, Arkansas; Oprah ⌐dent from East Senior High School, ...e, Tennessee.

I REGION V ORATORICAL CONTEST
Winner of 1970 Region V Oratorical Contest - Miss Oprah Gail Winfrey - from Nashville, Tenn. Left, Tennessee State Director of Education, Brother William C. Anderson, right, Brother J. Garrick Hardy - Region V Director of Education.

A clipping Oprah made of the newspaper article on her victory at the Elks Club Oratorical Contest.

Vernon persuaded her to enter a speech contest sponsored by the local Elks Club. Naturally, Oprah won. The prize was a partial scholarship to Tennessee State University. Because the college is located in Nashville, she could live at home and commute to her classes. Oprah enrolled as a speech and drama major.

"I hated, hated, hated, college," says Oprah. Why? Perhaps because she and her classmates had different opinions on many issues, she found college life difficult. In the 1960s and 1970s, blacks in America were struggling for basic civil rights. In those days, racism, or ill-treatment of blacks because of their skin color, was more frequent. Blacks were not allowed to attend the same schools, eat at the same restaurants, or use the same bathrooms and water fountains as whites in many parts of the country. Many blacks who were angry about racial injustice called for "black power" and separation from whites.

Oprah has always felt deep respect for those who fought battles for civil rights. She often refers gratefully to strong African-American women of earlier generations, such as Sojourner Truth, Fannie Lou Hamer, and Madame C. J. Walker. "I believe those women are a part of my legacy [heritage] and the bridges that I crossed to get where I am today." Still, Oprah did not view race in the same way as many of her classmates at the mostly-black college. She explains, "Everybody was angry for four years...It was 'in' to be angry. Whenever there was any conversation on race, I was on the other side, maybe because I never felt the kind of repression [prejudiced treatment] other black people are exposed to. I've not come up against obvious racism that I know of. I don't think, act, or live my life in racial terms." To make her point Oprah quotes the Reverend Jesse Jackson, a national civil rights leader: "Excellence is the best deterrent [defense] to racism." Or, in Oprah's words, "I am proud to be a black woman. I try to be the best at what I do. I always have, since the first grade. When you are the best, it is hard for people to keep you down."

Oprah was also different from her classmates in other ways. While they were simply students, she was

Walking down the runway at the "Miss Black America" pageant.

completing her courses and pursuing her career.

In 1972, Oprah won the "Miss Black Nashville" and "Miss Black Tennessee" contests, although she lost her bid for the "Miss Black America Contest." How did she win these titles? Oprah says that in those days she had "a marvelous figure," but that is hardly the only quality that led her to victory. Each contest included a talent and personality section. In those areas, Oprah was unbeatable. For one thing, she didn't give typical answers, as the other women did. She had lied often while living with her mother. But during her years in Nashville, Oprah had become convinced that telling the truth was always the best. So when one judge asked her what she would do if she won a million dollars, she burst out, "I'd be a spending fool!" Another contestant replied that she would give all the money to the poor. The judges voted for honesty.

In 1973, during her freshman year at college, WLAC, a local CBS television station, offered her a job. At first she said no, thinking that her schoolwork was more important. The station kept calling, and a speech professor persuaded her to take the job. He explained that jobs with CBS were the reason people went to college in the first place!

Oprah appeared on television as a reporter and

Oprah was only twenty years old when she got her first job in television.

anchor [news reader] on weekends and studied during the week. Vernon was proud of his daughter, but he didn't see her success as a reason to relax his rules. Oprah was the only reporter at the station who still had a curfew.

During Oprah's senior year in college in 1976, she was offered a job with the ABC television station in Baltimore. She would co-anchor the evening news.

That would make her one of the "stars" of the most important prime-time news show. She would also have to move away from home and drop out of school just one credit short of her diploma. She decided to take the job. Her career was really on its way!

Vernon was proud of his daughter, but he never stopped hoping that she would complete her degree. Even when she had achieved huge success with "The Oprah Winfrey Show," he continued to nag her about finishing college. Years later as a famous star, Oprah returned to Tennessee State University to do the last required course and senior project. In 1986, she graduated. Once again Vernon Winfrey had triumphed. As Oprah says, "He knew what he wanted and expected, and he would take nothing less."

Oprah enjoys her success.

4

It Was Like Breathing To Me

In 1977, signs around Baltimore asked, "What's an Oprah?" The local ABC station, WJZ, was advertising its new star. At the same time, Oprah herself was asking another question: "What am I doing here?" Oprah was only 22, and she had very little experience in writing the news and reporting it on the air. But by 1977, stations around the country had begun to feel pressure from the civil rights and women's movements.

At this time almost all television reporters and newscasters were white and male. The stations rushed to change their image, looking for minorities [blacks and other non-whites] and women. Oprah was in the right field at the right time. She knew that in Baltimore, as at the Nashville station, she was a "token"—the single minority hired to make the station appear fair. But, as Oprah says, "I was one happy token."

Oprah was happy, but scared and not really prepared. She now believes that "I had no business anchoring the news in a major market." She had no time to work her way up, gradually perfecting her skills. Instead, she had to learn her craft in public—on the air!

In addition, Oprah did not feel comfortable with some of the basic rules of reporting. A journalist is supposed to hide all emotions, giving the public just the facts without any personal opinions or reactions. Also, a reporter investigates the story without regard for the people who are involved in it.

But Oprah could not do that. She has always been an open, loving person. While reporting a tragedy, she would break in with "Wow! Isn't that terrible!" or other comments. As Oprah says, "I wasn't really cut

Oprah interviewing Tony Randall for WJZ-TV, Baltimore.

out for the news. I'd have to fight back the tears if a story was too sad." Also, she could not put any distance between herself and the people she was interviewing. She was always more concerned about the people involved than in reporting the story itself.

The station management was not happy with Oprah's approach. One crisis came after Oprah was sent to cover a fire. The station wanted Oprah to interview a woman whose children had died in the burning house. Oprah refused, but gave in when she was told that she was in danger of losing her job. Following the interview, though, Oprah apologized on the air for bothering the woman during her time of sorrow.

After a few months, WJZ removed Oprah from the news show. They decided that she needed a new "look," so they sent her to a fancy beauty salon in New York for a makeover. "If you are black and walk into a place where everybody's speaking French," says Oprah, "run in the opposite direction." That comment gives one a good idea of the results of her makeover. The salon had no experience with black hair. They used a lot of harsh chemicals. Oprah explains, "I kept telling them: 'Excuse me, the lotion is beginning to burn a little.' It wasn't burning—it was flaming!" A week later, she was bald. "There were no wigs big enough for my head," she says. "It's 24 1/2 inches around—so I had to walk around wearing scarves."

What does a bald, out-of-work anchorwoman do? She cried a lot, and kept on hoping. The hoping worked, because at this, the lowest point in Oprah's life, her big break was about to happen.

After a few months, WJZ reassigned Oprah to a morning show called "People Are Talking." "People Are Talking" was a talk show. Oprah could now do something she could not do on the news show. She could be herself, talk to the guests, and express real feelings. She could break down the formal wall between reporter and subject. "They put me on the talk show just to get rid of me," Oprah explains, "but it was really my saving grace. The first day I did it I thought, 'This is what I really should have been doing all along.'" The new format came so naturally to her, she says, "It was like breathing to me." With Oprah as co-host, the ratings for "People Are Talking" soared.

It was during this time in Baltimore that Oprah met one of her closest friends. Gayle King Bumpus, another WJZ employee, stayed at Oprah's house during a blizzard one night. Oprah and Gayle stayed up until 4 A.M. talking. Today, in spite of their incredibly busy lives (Gayle is a newscaster in Connecticut), Oprah and Gayle talk on the phone two or three times a day.

Oprah is the godmother of Gayle's two children.

In 1984, Oprah's career entered its next stage. Debra DiMaio, an associate producer on "People Are Talking," was searching for a job as a producer. She sent tapes of her work, including some of Oprah's shows, to a station in Chicago. Debra got the job, and so did Oprah! She took over a show called "A.M.

Chicago" that had always scored badly in the ratings. After only six weeks on the air, "A.M. Chicago" had more viewers in that city than "The Phil Donahue Show." "Donahue" was also located in Chicago and was one of the most popular national talk shows. In just seven months, "A.M. Chicago" was doing so well that its length was increased from thirty minutes to an hour. In September 1985, the show was renamed "The Oprah Winfrey Show." A year later, the show went "national" and was shown all across the country instead of just in Chicago. Oprah became the first black woman to host a national show aimed at both a black and white audience.

The nationwide "Oprah Winfrey Show" soon had twice as many viewers as any other talk show. The show also began to receive many awards. In 1987, the show won three daytime Emmy awards—for Outstanding Talk/Service Program, Outstanding

Oprah adds another Emmy to her collection.

Direction, and Outstanding Host. Five more Emmys have followed. In 1988, Oprah received the International Radio and Television Society's "Broadcaster of the Year Award." She is the youngest person ever honored with this title.

In November of that year, Oprah took more control of her show by buying it from the network. Part of the deal was a guarantee that ABC would carry the show for at least five more years. Oprah now jokes that she bought the show just to give herself an extra week's vacation. Still, she knows that the purchase made history. She is the first woman to own and produce her own talk show. She describes her excitement when the deal went through: "I was in my room at the Bel Air Hotel in Los Angeles…killing flies because I had left the windows open. I had a towel and was swinging it around the room when Jeff came in and told me we got ownership of the show…I went

The HARPO studios occupy one whole city block.

screaming down the hall when it hit me!"

The deal was made by HARPO Productions, Inc., the production company Oprah had formed in 1986. In addition to producing "The Oprah Winfrey Show," HARPO also makes television specials and movies. It is headquartered in a huge building that occupies an entire city block in downtown Chicago. After a great deal of repairs and improvements, the HARPO Building became a completely modern studio. It is the largest in the Midwest. The building contains offices for Oprah and her staff, as well as three sound stages where "The Oprah Winfrey Show" and other shows are taped. Oprah is only the third woman, and the first black woman, ever to own a television studio.

A few years before, in 1985, Oprah's career expanded into a whole new area. While producer Quincy Jones was in Chicago on business, he was relaxing in his hotel room watching television. After only a few minutes of "The Oprah Winfrey Show," Quincy realized that Oprah was perfect for the role of Sofia in the movie *The Color Purple*. Oprah had already read the novel by Alice Walker on which the movie is based. She loved it! When she finished reading, she knelt down and prayed, "Dear God, find me a way to get into this movie." Oprah says she would have done any job at all—even water girl. Instead, she was chosen for a starring role. In fact, she was nominated for an Academy Award for her very first movie.

Oprah didn't win, but her fine acting led to a part in *Native Son* and a starring role in a miniseries, *The Women of Brewster Place*. Both films are based on novels by African-American writers—Richard Wright and Gloria Naylor. *The Women of Brewster Place* was produced by HARPO. Oprah wants her company to bring other stories of black life to the screen. She has bought the rights to *Beloved* by Toni Morrison, a novel describing a woman's escape and recovery from slavery. HARPO will also make a film of *Kaffir Boy*, the autobiography of Mark Mathabane, who grew up in the racist state of South Africa, and *Their Eyes Were Watching God*, a novel of a black girl's coming of age

Native Son.

by Zora Neale Hurston. To Oprah, making films based on important works of African and African-American literature is an educational and spiritual mission. "Good film is one of the best ways to raise consciousness," she explains.

In 1990, Oprah also turned the *The Women of*

Brewster Place into a weekly television series called "Brewster Place." Again, she aimed to educate as well as to entertain. "Most people out there have no contact with black people ever. Their only images are the ones portrayed on TV," Oprah says. "There's a whole reality outside of what most people know, where the black community functions on its own, where people own businesses, where people care about prosperity and their children and pay their taxes. The point of having your own company is that you can show that."

That is the philosophy of Oprah Winfrey: learn yourself, teach others. And with her own company, she can show the rest of the country the lives, hopes, troubles, and dreams of the African-American community.

"The Oprah Winfrey Show."

5

I'm Still Learning

Each day "The Oprah Winfrey Show" has a different theme: drug and alcohol abuse, childhood friends, celebrity interviews, adoption, racism in college, and so forth. People who have experiences relating to the topic are invited, as are experts in the field. The guests discuss the day's subject, answering questions from the audience. The host guides the discussion. This is a normal format, one that is used by hundreds of talk shows around the country every day.

Although "The Oprah Winfrey Show" discusses the same issues as other shows, it does not have the same atmosphere. That's because of Oprah. The *Washington Post* called her "...the kind of brassy neighbor who barges into your house and immediately goes to the refrigerator for a little Cheese Whiz and bacon dip. And you love her for it." Oprah herself says, "I'm not afraid of being...human, making mistakes." She adds, "I ask questions that I want the answer to, and I know that if I'm thinking of a question, somebody else out there is asking it too."

She says that there is "no such thing as an embarrassing moment" on her show. "In order for something to be embarrassing you have to feel alone or rejected in some way. I know that there is nothing that could possibly happen to me that hasn't already happened to a million other people. So if I trip and fall flat on my face or forget what I'm saying in the middle of a sentence, or if my pantyhose fall down to my knees when I'm walking across the stage, all of which has happened to me, no big deal."

"The Oprah Winfrey Show" is always interesting because no one ever knows what Oprah will say or do next. Once she kicked her shoes off, telling the audience, "My feet are killing me." Another time she held hands and cried with an elderly black man as he described a lynching. During a quiet spell in her love life, she told everyone that "Mr. Right" was on his way. "He's in Africa, walking." On a show featuring husbands who refused to go for marriage counseling, she offered to pay for the therapy. One startled husband then agreed to go! On Oprah's most famous show, a guest explained that she had been raped as a child. Oprah threw her arms around the woman and started to cry. For the very first time, she revealed her own childhood abuse. More than 800 viewers called to say that the show helped them face their own past experiences.

Helping others is one of the goals of "The Oprah Winfrey Show" and of its host. Oprah says that she wants "...to recognize my full potential as a human

Oprah's warm, honest personality has made her very popular with talk show viewers.

being on this planet and to help other people do the same." She adds, "People watch our show and realize they're not alone. Whatever problems you have, there's somebody out there who has overcome something similar in his or her life. And if they can, you can too."

Oprah also wants viewers to realize that "you are responsible for your life." Once a guest complained that her husband didn't "let" her do something. The audience immediately interrupted her, "You are an adult. You don't need permission," they said. Oprah nodded. "The Oprah Winfrey audience," she said. "They know about responsibility."

So does Oprah. Perhaps that's why she's so busy. There's so much she wants to accomplish. Her day "...starts with working out at 6:00 A.M. and ends somewhere around 8:00 P.M." According to Oprah, "a typical day for me would involve: makeup and hair, show preparation by a producer, greeting the studio audience, taping two Oprah Winfrey shows, conducting HARPO business meetings, planning, etc. and finally (hopefully) retiring at home with a good book."

During the "show preparation," Oprah talks with one of her staff members, who briefs her on each guest's ideas and background. The staff often suggests questions for Oprah to ask, although Oprah rejects some questions and adds many of her own. But the ideas for each show come from both the staff and from Oprah herself. Oprah sometimes attends "focus" meetings where ordinary viewers are asked what they would like to see on the show; other ideas come from Oprah's wide reading.

Oprah tries not to skip her early morning workout because she struggles with a weight problem. Oprah's size has been a frequent topic on her television show.

Oprah has learned to love herself no matter what her weight.

In a career where almost all stars are thin, Oprah proved that big can be beautiful. Nevertheless, she was not satisfied with her appearance. She tried all kinds of diet and exercise plans. For a long time, none of them worked. Then one day Oprah realized that she eats when she gets nervous or upset. She once explained to her audience, "I'll be angry but I won't say anything. Three days later the anger will be in my thighs."

In recent years, Oprah has succeeded in losing weight. On an amazing show in November, 1988, she walked on stage pulling a wagon piled with 67 pounds of beef fat—the amount of weight she had lost. It was a great victory, but Oprah knows that it was just one battle, not the whole war. Her weight has gone up and down in the months following that show. Oprah believes that she will only win by loving herself enough to take proper care of herself. She says, "Learning to love yourself is the greatest love of all; it's not just a song. It's the truth. I know because I'm still learning."

Oprah also sees loving herself as the key to healthy relationships with others. "If you love yourself," she explains, "you attract people who are loving to you." As a teenager and a young adult, Oprah was still recovering from the abuse of her childhood years. She often found herself in unhappy romances. She cried for days when William Taylor, a boyfriend from her Nashville years, broke up with her. At the end of a four-year relationship with a man in Baltimore, she even threatened to kill herself. "Can you believe that?" she comments. "Never, never again."

She is now in a happy romance with Stedman Graham, a former basketball player whom she calls "an overwhelmingly decent man. He has made me realize a lot of the things that were missing in my life, like the sharing that goes on between two people." Stedman has worked as the director of Athletes Against Drugs. He now runs a public relations firm. Although the gossip newspapers continually report that Oprah and Stedman are about to marry, they are keeping their plans private.

Out on the town with Stedman.

But privacy for Oprah, one of the most famous women in America, is hard to find. Perhaps because Oprah comes into their living rooms every day, or perhaps just because she is warm and loving, her fans are not afraid to talk to her. Once Oprah was having dinner with Stedman. A fan came over, sat down, and chatted. The fan felt so welcome that she even ordered dessert—which Oprah ended up paying for! Viewers approach her on the street. Rather than being in awe of a famous star and too shy to speak, they say, "Wait right there. I'll get a pen for an autograph."

Oprah does sign autographs, reciting Bible verses to herself when she tires of it. She always tries to be patient—and to keep her sense of humor. "Being famous is fun, and if you ever take it to mean any more than that, you're taking it too seriously!" She also tries to deal with the tough parts of being a celebrity. "People assume you've changed," she says.

"They know if they were famous for three minutes they would lose their minds, and they assume I've lost mine. The least [little] thing and they say, 'You're too good for me now.'" That attitude can hurt even a famous star.

But Oprah's best friends know that she will always be completely loyal to them. Aside from Gayle King Bumpus, she is also close to Akosua Busia, an actress who appeared with her in *The Color Purple*, and to author Maya Angelou, whom Oprah calls, "my mother, my sister, my teacher, and my friend." Angelou was one of Oprah's heroes as a young woman. She, too, was raised on a farm in the South by her grandmother and the stories of her childhood are similar to Oprah's in many ways.

Oprah also sees the employees of HARPO as friends. She spends many hours with them, and she never presents herself as "the boss." One of her co-

Oprah and Maya Angelou.

workers comments, "She is a democratic person. Oprah treats everyone the same. When she walks on the set, she greets the dolly grip [one of the stage workers] the same as she'd greet a producer." Oprah herself believes that "I'm building a family here. I hire people with the intention of letting them move up and grow into being everything they can be, from the receptionist on down."

Oprah also remains close to Vernon Winfrey, although they live in different cities and cannot spend much time together. She has tried to shower him with presents, but he has only accepted a few. The only thing he ever asked for was tickets to a Mike Tyson fight, which Oprah happily provided. She has also made peace with her mother. Oprah bought Vernita an apartment and supports her financially.

Oprah is, of course, fabulously wealthy. She lives in a huge apartment with a spectacular view of

Although she is a smart businesswoman, Oprah prefers to use her money to better the world.

Lake Michigan. The apartment has a master bedroom opening into a "media room" with a giant TV and a stereo system. There are many other rooms, including a library, a dining room, and guest rooms. The apartment is decorated with many works by African-American artists, as well as sculpture from Africa.

Yet Oprah's wealth means much more to her than the possessions she can buy with it. Oprah uses her money, as well as her time and energy, to work for a better future. She has contributed thousands of dollars to help battered women and victims of AIDS, the disease that recently killed her half-brother. She has also donated money to South African freedom-fighter Nelson Mandela, and provided funds to feed an entire South African village. The Better Boys Foundation for inner-city kids receives donations from Oprah, as do many women's shelters. She also gave a million dollars to Morehouse College in

Atlanta, and endowed ten full scholarships to Tennessee State University in her father's name.

Her concern with education comes from her own beginnings on a poor farm in Mississippi and in the inner-city of Milwaukee. "I saw a way out," she says. "That's why education is so important. It exposes a way out. You get to read about, if not see, a sort of place where life can be better. I always believed that sort of life was possible for me. Your belief combined with your willingness to fulfill your dreams is what makes success possible."

No doubt about it—success is what Oprah Winfrey has. "Ain't it something?" she asks. "I feel as good as you can feel and still live!"

Bibliography

Interviews and Correspondence

HARPO Productions, Inc. Statistics and unpublished personal biographies, 15 September, 1990.

Winfrey, Oprah. Written interview with author, 5 October, 1990.

Books

King, Norman. *Everybody Loves Oprah!–Her Story.* New York: William Morrow & Company, 1987.

Articles

Barthel, Joan. "Here Comes Oprah!" *Ms.* (August 1986): 46.

Colander, Pat. "Oprah Winfrey's Odyssey: Talk-Show Host to Mogul." *New York Times* (March 12, 1989): 31.

Edwards, Audrey. "Stealing the Show." *Essence* (October 1986): 51.

Harmetz, Aljean. "Learning to Live With Runaway Fame." *New York Times* (May 18, 1986): 19.

Littwin, Susan. "Oprah Opens Up." *TV Guide* (May 5, 1990): 4.

Morgan, Thomas. "Troubled Girl's Evolution into an Oscar Nominee." *New York Times* (March 4, 1986): 21.

Robertson, Nan. "Actresses' Varied Roads to the Color Purple." *New York Times* (February 13, 1986).

Taylor, Susan. "An Intimate Talk With Oprah." *Essence* (August 1987): 57.

Whitaker, Charles, "TV's New Daytime Darling." *The Saturday Evening Post* (July/August 1987): 43.

Zoglin, Richard. "Lady With a Calling." *Time* (August 8, 1988): 63.

Index